Joseph Alden, John Andrew, John Filmer

The Burial of the First Born

a tale for children

Joseph Alden, John Andrew, John Filmer

The Burial of the First Born
a tale for children

ISBN/EAN: 9783337023843

Printed in Europe, USA, Canada, Australia, Japan

Cover: Foto ©Andreas Hilbeck / pixelio.de

More available books at **www.hansebooks.com**

THE

BURIAL OF THE FIRST BORN,

A

TALE FOR CHILDREN.

BY

JOSEPH ALDEN, D. D.

AUTHOR OF "THE CARDINAL-FLOWER," "THE LOST LAMB," ETC.

BOSTON:

J. E. TILTON AND COMPANY,

161 WASHINGTON STREET.

1863.

CONTENTS.

6 CONTENTS.

BURIAL OF THE FIRST BORN.

CHAPTER I.

THE DEATH OF THE FIRST BORN.

Lights might have been seen burning during the whole night in the house of Mr. Ashton. At times they passed rapidly from room to room, and then were steady in the chambers occupied by Mr. and Mrs. Ashton and their children. Long before daylight, all movement had ceased, and a dim light only shone from the windows of Mr. and Mrs. Ashton's apartment.

If you could then have looked into that chamber, you would have seen a sad sight. On the bed laid the lifeless body of Henry, their first born child. He was about eight years of age. In the evening, he went to bed with his little sister, who was two years younger than himself, in his usual health: before morning, he was a corpse.

The mother has thrown herself on the bed beside her child, and is weeping bitterly. The father is sitting, with the yet warm hand of his lifeless son in his, with tearless agony.

The day at length dawned. How unwelcome was the light to those broken-hearted watchers! The sun arose, and through the eastern window cast his rays on the face of the sleeper who was never to waken more till the sun had ceased its risings.

In the morning, the sad news spread rapidly through the village. Henry Ashton was dead! Many a young heart was chilled, and many an old one felt heavy, and heaved a sigh, for Henry was the favorite of the young and the old. His gentle and affectionate disposition, his quick intelligence, and respectful manner, secured the esteem of all who knew him. All were anxious to hear the particulars of his sudden and untimely death.

Just as Mr. and Mrs. Ashton were about to retire for the night, they looked in, as they were accustomed to do, upon their children, who slept in an adjoining chamber. Henry was awake, and said, with difficulty, in a whisper, "Papa, I can't speak." This effort was followed by that hoarse cough, so terrible to the ear of the experienced parent. All the remedies in their power were applied, but in vain. The disease gained upon the darling boy. It was the croup, in its most dangerous form.

Difficulty of breathing increased. After partial recovery from a violent paroxysm, his father said to him, in a tone of calm agony, "My son, I am afraid you must die." The look which was given in reply, was as though a two-edged sword had passed through the father's heart.

"Papa, can't you help me?" whispered the dying boy.

The father shook his head.

"Can't you pray for me?"

Again the father shook his head. Henry attempted to speak again, but was unable to, even in a whisper. He then closed his eyes, and lay as still as his laborious breathing would allow, for about twenty minutes. Was he praying? The Maker of his spirit only knows.

At the end of that time another paroxysm took place.

"Papa — do — pray — for me," gasped the sufferer. In a few moments his sufferings were over.

Why did not his papa pray for him? will be the question of the reader. I will tell you. His Papa was not a Christian. He was not even a believer in the Bible. In the madness of his heart he had said that religion was a delusion, and the Bible a cunningly devised fable. The voice of prayer had never been heard under his roof. The Bible was not read there. The Saviour was not spoken of there. The children were carefully instructed in all things pertaining to this life, but left wholly in ignorance with reference to the life to come.

But where was the mother? Can a mother hear her child utter her name, and not teach it to lisp the infant's prayer? Can a mother suffer a child to remain ignorant of its Father who is in heaven? Can a mother fail to tell her child of that Saviour who said, " Suffer little children to come unto me, and forbid them not ? "

Alas! Mrs. Ashton was one of those gentle, yielding beings who are controled by others. She was not pious, but she belonged to a family in which religion was respected, and some of its forms observed. She gave **her** heart to Ashton without inquiring what were his views on the subject which should receive our chief attention at all times and in every action of our lives.

After they were married she came gradually to entertain his views. Still when she became a mother, and when her child began to speak, she taught him the prayer she herself had been taught by her departed mother. When this came to the knowledge of her husband, he for the first time treated her with harshness, and commanded her to cease from teaching " superstition" to his child. She yielded; it was with sorrow, but she yielded, and God was banished from that house. Still God did not withhold his blessing from that house. Life, health, food, abundance was meted out to that household, but in vain. The goodness of God did not lead them to repentance. Then he put forth his hand, and smote their first born, and hid him in the grave.

Reader, do you belong to a praying family? Have you parents who teach you the way of life? Have you parents who can pray for you? Who has made you to differ from those worse than orphans whose parents, even in the hour of death, cannot pray for them?

CHAPTER II.

THE FUNERAL.

KIND friends offered that assistance which makes the preparations for a funeral in the country so different from those in the city.

"When will you have the funeral appointed?" said Mr. Ames, a venerable deacon of the church, who had volunteered to superintend the arrangements connected with the burial.

"I shall bury him to-morrow in the afternoon," said Mr. Ashton in a husky voice.

"At what hour shall the funeral be appointed?" said Mr. Ames.

"At no hour. I do not need the assistance of the priest. If our neighbors wish to go with us to the grave, I have no objection; indeed I shall be glad to have them."

"Do n't you mean to have the minister?" said deacon Ames in astonishment.

"No."

"You had better."

"I know my own views and feelings best."

"Well, let us have him for the sake of the people if not for your own sake."

"We shall bury our child to-morrow at two o'clock. If our neighbors wish to go with us to the grave, **and to** assist in covering him, I shall **be glad to have them do** so. But let them bring no priest with them, and let them expect no superstitious rites."

This was said in a tone which discouraged all further solicitation on the part of deacon Ames. He retired with a sad heart, and in reply to questions respecting the funeral, he was obliged to state the conversation which **had** taken place between himself and the bereaved father.

A feeling of grief and horror pervaded the **community.** Such **open** defiance of God, even when his hand lay heavy upon the offender, they had never witnessed. In this feeling the children fully sympathized. **They** could **not** bear to think of having their beloved Henry carried to his grave with no prayer offered, and no address made to those who wept his loss.

Much conversation took place both among **the old and the young as to what** should **be done.**

2

At length a number of the children of their own accord held a meeting, and appointed two of their number to go and persuade Mr. Ashton to have the minister come and offer a prayer and make an ddress to them over the coffin of their beloved playmate.

James Wilson and George Ward were appointed on this committee; James because he was the most intimate friend of Henry, and George for his ready command of language.

James and George went on their way with boldness till they came near the house. Then they made frequent stops, and held consultations. It was finally agreed that James should enter the house first, and George should prefer the request with which they were charged to Mr. Ashton.

They entered the door. Mr. Ashton was sitting in the hall. No tear was in his eye. No traces of tears were on his cheeks; but there were marks of grief upon his brow deeper than are ever graven there when the heart can cast its burden upon the Lord.

"Do you wish to see Henry?" said Mr. Ashton.

" Yes, sir," said George, quite encouraged by the softness of his tone.

He led them to the room, where in the repose of death the late active limbs of their companion lay. They wept freely as they stood beside the coffin. Mr. Ashton stood by their side, and now for the first time the tears came into his eyes. James noticed it, and whispered to George to begin.

" Wont you let Mr. Jones come and pray for us, and talk to us here before Henry is buried? Henry used to love him," said George, giving Mr. Ashton at the same time the eloquent look of genuine feeling.

" Henry used to love him," repeated Mr. Ashton, not quite in a tone of inquiry.

" Yes, sir; I have heard him say so a great many times."

There was silence for some time while both the boys looked earnestly and imploringly into Mr. Ashton's countenance, and then on that of the departed one.

" You may go to Mr. Jones," said Mr. Ashton, " and say to him, that I wish to have him come and talk to the children and pray for them at two o'clock to-morrow, when Henry will be buried."

" Thank you, sir," said George, and ere he took his leave, he applied his lips to those of his departed friend. **In so** doing tears fell on that cold cheek. Mr. Ashton noticed them. He did not wipe them away.

The boys returned to those who had sent **them, and** reported the success of their mission. It was quickly told to their parents, and all rejoiced so far as joy could be felt in connexion with so sad a bereavement.

At the appointed hour, all the inhabitants of the village assembled. The children were allowed to fill the room in which the body lay **and the** adjacent hall. Parents and adults filled the remaining rooms, and formed a large group before **the door.**

The discourse of the pastor was mainly addressed to the young, yet it caused tears to course down many a furrowed cheek. He **prayed** distinctly and fervently for the afflicted parents, and their remaining child. This was evidently grateful to the mother, and called forth no expression of disapprobation from the **father.**

The last prayer was offered, and the body was borne to the grave amid weeping such as had rarely been witnessed before. The coffin was lowered into the grave, the earth was lightly thrown in by friendly hands, the thanks of the mourners were rendered to the attendants, and all returned sadly to their homes.

CHAPTER III.

THE PRAYER MEETING.

So deep was the impression made by the religious services of the funeral that, before the children left the grave-yard, they had agreed to meet, an hour before sunset, at the old oak tree and hold a prayer meeting. The old oak tree was in a grove just behind the school-house. It was a very large tree, and the ends of the lower branches came down almost to the ground, thus forming a very secluded place, and one very suitable for the meeting in question. James and George, the two boys who have already been introduced to the reader, had often prayed together there. They had been taught to pray by their parents, and by the spirit of God.

The next thing to be done after the meeting was agreed upon, was to invite little Susan Ashton, the sister of the deceased, and if possible to secure her attendance. George undertook the task. He went to Mr. Ashton's

and found Susan sitting on the door-step, looking over the **books** her brother had left her,
not reading them, but thinking of the **times**
when Henry **had** read them **to** her. She
thought of his great kindness to her, for he
loved his **little sister very much,** and took great
care of her; then she thought of some times
when she had not treated him well, when (if
the truth must be told) she had quarreled
with him, and it made her heart ache sorely.

"We are going to have a prayer meeting
at the old oak tree, an hour before sunset,"
said George **to** Susan, "**and** we want you to
come."

"A **prayer** meeting at the oak tree?" said
Susan, **as** though she did not know what sort
of a thing it was.

"Yes," said George; "we wish to have you
come very much, because we are all so sorry for
you."

"I will ask mother," said Susan.

At that moment Mrs. Ashton came to **the**
door. Her eyes **were red** with weeping.
George did not wait for Susan to ask her, but
made the request himself.

"**Oh, yes,**" said **Mrs. Ashton;** "she may

go, but," as though recollecting herself, " you must ask Mr. Ashton."

Susan went in to ask her father, and George went in with her.

" Papa," said she, " may I go to the prayer meeting?"

" What prayer meeting?" said Mr. Ashton, in rather a stern tone. Susan turned towards George, who answered, " We are going to hold a prayer meeting, sun about an hour high, at the old oak tree. As it is chiefly on Susan's account, we should be glad to have her come."

Mr. Ashton was silent for a long time, and looked steadily on the floor. At length George said, " will you please let her come?" Mr. Ashton replied with a nod. George and Susan retired from his presence.

" Sister Jane will stop for you," said George; " do you be all ready when she comes along."

About a dozen boys and girls assembled at the place of meeting at the appointed hour. They seated themselves on the green grass, and James read a chapter in the Bible. They then sung an hymn. James then made a solemn and affecting prayer. It was not made up of petitions which he had heard others use. It was confined almost wholly to thoughts brought to mind by the peculiar circumstances in which they were placed. They then sung another hymn and a little girl prayed. Her prayer consisted wholly of petitions in behalf of Susan.

Susan had hardly left the house to go with Jane to the meeting, before her father felt a strong desire to follow her. He rose up with the purpose of doing so, and then he thought it would not be proper to break in upon the privacy of the young worshippers. So he sat down again. But his thoughts were with the little circle at the old oak tree, and at length his desires to go there were so strong that he could not keep his seat. He said to himself that he would walk in that direction and be ready to meet Susan on her way home. He kept on walking in that direction till he came to the grove. He entered it and went towards the tree but not in the path. He drew near to the tree. The thick bushes concealed him from view. They were just closing a hymn. Then there was silence. Then he heard the low, solemn voice of George in prayer. The prayer was very short, but very much to the

purpose. It contained petitions for the bereaved Susan, and especially for her father and
mother. The heart of Ashton was softened as
he gazed upon the kneeling forms of that little
band, and listened to the tones of that child-
like prayer.

They arose from their knees, and a few
words were spoken to them by George so simple, so earnest, so full of sympathy, that the
heart of the strong man gave way. He sunk
to the earth and lay prostrate there, while tears
flowed copiously from eyes unused to weep.

The children departed **for** their homes, **and**
silence reigned in the grove. Not a leaf
stirred. Not a bird flitted by, not a note was
heard. The deep stillness added to the impression already made on Ashton's heart. He
arose and went to the deserted place of prayer.
There he believed and felt that there **was a**
prayer hearing God. He kneeled and prayed
that God, whose government he had denied,
and whose authority he had despised, would
soften his heart and make him like **a** little child.

He arose from his knees **and** saw a book
lying on the turf. He opened it. It was
James' Bible, which he had forgotten. He

will not forget it long. He will miss it when he begins to prepare for bed, if not before; for he never goes to bed without reading a chapter in his Bible. It was the dying gift of his mother, now in heaven, and he has never forgotten to keep her charge to read in it every day.

Mr. Ashton read the pages of that, to him, strange book, till the shadows of evening began to fall. He then closed it, and placing it where he found it, returned to his desolate dwelling.

CHAPTER IV.

OPINIONS RESPECTING THE PRAYER MEETING.

THE old oak tree prayer meeting was not a secret, and it occasioned a good deal of remark.

"Well, deacon Ames, have you heard about the bush prayer meeting?" said Mr. Rockwell as he called at the Deacon's the next morning. Mr. Rockwell had a great fear of persons young and old being righteous over much. He himself always took care to err on the safe side.

"About what?" said deacon Ames gravely, by his manner rebuking Mr. Rockwell's levity.

"Why about the meeting the children had in the woods."

"I have heard that they held a prayer meeting in their grove last evening and was glad to hear it."

"Well, I declare I did n't expect to hear you say so; I thought you were a greater friend to order than that."

"I am told that it was a very orderly meeting, quite as much so as if a minister had been there."

" They are too young to manage such things."

" They are not too young to die, it seems," said the deacon solemnly.

Mr. Rockwell changed the conversation and soon took his leave. He could never get along to his mind with deacon Ames. The deacon would never dispute or argue with him, but had such a solemn way of saying the truth that he seldom felt comfortable after an interview.

Mr. Rockwell went from deacon Ames' to Mr. Graham's store. " What do you think ?" said he to Mr. Graham ; " deacon Ames approves of these children's meetings, and if he carries the minister with him, I don't know what we shall come to."

" It was a foolish and improper thing," said Mr. Graham, referring to the meeting at the oak tree. He was called away to attend a customer, and the conversation between him and Mr. Rockwell went no further.

Mr. Graham's son Robert, a lad of about nine years of age, was in the store, and heard his father's remark. Robert was not at the meeting. He had heard about it, and was sorry that he did not go. He wondered what his father could mean by saying it was a foolish and improper thing.

Robert had a good head, and made a pretty good use of it. He was accustomed to think out the reasons of things. He tried to think out the reasons of the above remark, but he could not do it. He felt very sure there must be good reasons for it, for his father was regarded as a man of sound judgment. "It must be so, if my father says so," said he to himself after a long season of thought; "but I cannot see why."

He then attempted to dismiss the matter from his thoughts, but without success. It would claim his attention. So he resolved that he would ask his father, why a children's prayer meeting in a beautiful and retired grove was a "foolish and improper thing."

He found no opportunity of talking to his father till evening. After dark, when the family were sitting in the piazza, looking out on the bright stars, and enjoying the cool summer breeze, when there was a pause in the conversation, Robert said to his father, "father, I have been thinking all day about what you said this morning to Mr. Rockwell, and I can't see the reason of it."

" What was it ?" said his father who did not recollect what he had said to Mr. Rockwell.

" Father said it was a foolish and improper thing for the children to have a prayer meeting. I have been trying, but I can't see why."

" You are too young to see the reasons of all things," said Mr. Graham, and he immediately began to converse with Mrs. Graham on another topic, giving Robert to understand that he did not wish to hear anything more on the subject.

" Papa is tired," thought Robert, " or wishes to talk about something else now. I will ask mother to-morrow."

During most of the forenoon of the next day, Robert was employed in doing errands for his mother, and had no good opportunity to speak to her, on the subject of the meeting, till afternoon. He had just begun to speak to her, when the minister came in. This defeated Robert's purpose for the time, but he was not sorry. He loved Mr. Jones, and loved to hear him talk, — he " talked so good," as the children use to say.

The death and funeral of Henry were natur-
ally made the subject of remark. Then Mr.
Jones mentioned the prayer meeting. "Now,"
thought Robert, "I shall learn what I wish to
know," for on religious subjects he had even
more confidence in the minister's opinions than
he had in his father's. To the disappointment
of Robert, Mr. Jones seemed to think very
differently from his father in relation to the
meeting. His eye now sparkled with pleasure
and now was moistened by a tear as he gave
Mrs. Graham an account of the meeting, and
expressed his strong hopes respecting the
results to which it might lead.

How did Mr. Jones know so much about the
meeting? Mr. Ashton had been to see him
to ask his counsel and his prayers, and from
him he had learned the particulars which have
been given to the reader. He said nothing
however to Mrs. Graham or to any one else
respecting Mr. Ashton's visit.

CHAPTER V.

MORE ABOUT THE PRAYER MEETING.

FOR some days after the death of Henry, the children of the school which he used to attend, were less lively and noisy in their sports, but before long you could not perceive any difference. Still Henry was not forgotten. Often when his class was called up to read and there was no Henry there, the thoughts of many would silently wander to his lonely resting place in the church yard. And often, when you might see a scholar with his eyes directed to his book, his thoughts had reference to Henry rather than to the lesson.

On the fourth day after the funeral, when school was dismissed, there was some difference of opinion as to what sport they should engage in. James Wilson proposed one and Simon Morton another. James' popularity caused his wishes to be followed at once by the great majority of the children. This vexed Simon, who was a bad tempered and by no means popular boy.

3*

"I should n't think," said he to James, "that folks as good as you pretend to be would play at all; I should think they **would have** meeting all the time."

This was said in a very insulting tone, **but** James paid no attention to it, though it placed him in an awkward position, as all the children kept silence to hear what he would say in reply. He said nothing. This encouraged Simon to continue his remarks.

"Mr. Minister," said he, "I do n't think it looks well for you to be playing with these here sinners; you had better be preaching."

James still paid no attention to the railer, remembering the words relating to the Saviour, "who when he was reviled, reviled not again."

The angry boy became still more angry because James kept cool.

"Come on, all hands, to prayer meeting," said he in a loud voice; "the Reverend Mr. James Wilson will hold a prayer meeting under the oak tree in the grove; so come on, all hands."

"You wicked boy," said Charlotte Gordon to him; "you ought to be ashamed of yourself."

This rebuke from the finest girl in the school

did make him ashamed, and he withdrew, making some remark which was not distinctly heard.

James clearly had the victory, but his feelings had been so much hurt that he did not feel like playing. The scholars sympathized with him, and they all went to their homes without their usual hour of play.

There was one girl who wished to have James reply to the implied charges brought against him by Simon. She thought that James was a very good boy, very good indeed: she should think he was a Christian only he loved to play as well as other boys did. She did not see how that could be if he were a Christian. And yet he was so good that she thought, on the whole, that he must be one. There was a difficulty which she wished to have removed. Several others entertained ideas somewhat similar, though they did not assume quite as definite a shape in their minds as in hers.

Nothing was said by James to relieve the difficulty. When Julia, for that was her name, went home, she resolved to propose it to her mother. She began by relating what had taken place between James and Simon after school. Her mother expressed a very warm approval of James' course, saying that he acted like a Christian.

"Mother," said Julia, "do you think that James is a Christian?"

"It is not for us to judge who are, and who are not Christians; but I have never seen or heard of any thing that would lead me to suppose that he was not a Christian."

"I do n't **know of but one** thing," said Julia with some hesitation.

"What is that?" said her mother with some solicitude lest she should hear something **to** James's disadvantage.

"He loves to play as well as the other boys, if not better," said Julia.

"Does he play on the Sabbath?"

"Oh no! I presume **not.**"

"**Does** he play in school?"

"**No,** ma'am, never. He scarcely ever looks **off** from his book **in** school."

"When does **he** play then?"

"After school, when the other boys and girls play."

"Is he ever harsh, or coarse, or unkind in his play?"

" No, ma'am."

" What is there about his playing then that is wrong?"

" I do n't know as there is anything — only — I did n't know as Christians ought to play at all."

" You are wanting, my dear," said her mother, " in correct ideas of religion. What do you suppose was God's design in making us capable of religion?"

" To save us, I suppose."

" Rather it was to make us happy. Do n't you suppose he desires to see us happy?"

" Yes, ma'am."

" God's commandments are only rules for securing our highest happiness. God's law does not forbid anything that will promote our real happiness. When God says, 'thou shalt love the Lord thy God with all thy heart, and thy neighbor as thyself,' he is only commanding us to be as happy as our nature will allow."

" But do n't religion require us to be sober?"

" Certainly it does. But we can be sober and yet partake of innocent recreation. We are commanded to rejoice evermore, but this does not forbid us to weep in affliction. True religion consists in doing every thing with reference to the will of God, seeking to please God in every thing, serving him in every thing."

"We can't serve God in playing — can we?"

"Yes, my dear, when it is God's will that we should play, then you serve him in playing. You know the Apostle says, 'whether ye eat or drink, or whatsoever you do, do all to the glory of God.' We do a thing for the glory of God when we do it with a desire to please him. What we want to know is just what God will be pleased to have us do each day and each hour. When he would have us pray, then if we pray we serve him in prayer; when he would have us study, then if we study we serve him in study; when he would have us take recreation and refreshment, then if we take them we serve him in recreation and refreshment.

"It is certainly for their health and happiness that children should play at proper times, and therefore it is their duty to do so. They are to play, as they are to do every thing else, in the fear of God."

" James does play in the fear of God, for he will never play with any of the boys if they say bad words, or if they get angry."

" I do not see that his being fond of play at the proper time is anything at all against him. Religion does not interfere with any source of real happiness — on the contrary it heightens every innocent joy."

CHAPTER VI.

MR. ASHTON'S VISIT TO THE PASTOR.

THE impression made upon the mind of little Susan by the pastor's address at the funeral was increased at the prayer meeting under the old oak tree. The solemn truths of religion were new to her mind. But of the feelings thereby awakened those of curiosity and wonder were perhaps the strongest.

" Papa, where do you think Henry is gone ?" said she, on the morning after the funeral as she sat with the father and mother at their cheerless breakfast.

" He is dead," said Mr. Ashton, affecting to misunderstand her question. His eyes met those of his wife, and the burning blushes that overspread their countenances showed that they both understood the full meaning of the question, and felt that it was one of awful import.

As soon as Mr. Ashton arose from the breakfast table he repaired to the house of the pastor. Mr. Jones found his heart deeply affected, while his ignorance in regard to the simplest principles of religion was very great. There was not a child in the Sabbath school who was not able to give him instruction on the subject of religion. And yet he was an intelligent and educated man, and had lived in a gospel land for more than forty years.

He had hated the truth; he had closed his eyes to the light. He had been present when the gospel was preached, but he had not heard it. In the house of God, when the message of mercy was delivered, his thoughts were busy with worldly topics, and though the words of the preacher fell on his external ear, they did not reach the ear of his spirit.

Mr. Jones gave him such counsel as was adapted to his case. The chief direction was that he should study the word of God. Till his deep ignorance in regard to God and the way of salvation was removed, he knew it would be impossible for him to become a Christian.

On his return from his visit to the pastor, Mr. Ashton shut himself up in his room, and spent the day in reading his long-neglected Bible, and in prayer. By the aid of the Spirit, the truth began to give light to his darkened

4

mind, and activity and power to his awakened
conscience. With the awful truths of eternity
clearly before his mind, the last words of his
dying boy were remembered, — "Papa, can't
you pray for me ;" and he knew, as he never
did before, the meaning of the term *agony*.
He had the terrible conviction that his child
was lost — that his father was the destroyer
of his soul !

But God had been kinder to little Henry
than his father knew of. He had caused the
faithful pastor to feel a peculiar interest in
him. The benignant countenance and bland
smile of the ingenuous pastor won Henry's
heart, and caused him to give earnest heed to
the words of instruction which were faithfully
given whenever an occasion offered.

And then God raised up for him a kind and
Christian friend in James Wilson. For months
before his death, his mind had become interested
in the subject of personal religion. He often
joined with James in prayer in the school-
house, when all the pupils had gone home, and
in the grove, " when none but God could hear."
Though he did not profess to have found the
Saviour, yet he gave so many indications of a

renewed heart that **on** reviewing them after his death, James could not **but** indulge the hope, that the Lord had prepared him for **heaven** before he took him from the earth.

What a comfort was it **to** James to be **able to** think **that he had in a measure** been faithful to the soul of his friend!

CHAPTER VII.

A VISIT OF SYMPATHY TO SUSAN.

"Mother," said Charlotte Gordon, "may I go and see Susan Ashton this afternoon?"

"I thought you were very much interested in your new books," said Mrs. Gordon.

"I am, very much indeed, but then I thought that Susan must be so lonesome that I had better go and see her for a little while."

Mrs. Gordon was pleased to see in her daughter this showing of sympathy for the afflicted. She knew that by cherishing such feelings and carrying them out into action she would become useful and happy. She cheerfully gave her the desired permission to go and visit Susan.

It was with considerable reluctance that Charlotte laid aside her books and prepared to go to Mr. Ashton's. She looked wistfully upon the very interesting book which she was reading, and asked herself, whether a visit to Susan to-morrow would not do almost as well;

but she thought of Henry in his grave and
Susan all alone, **and felt** ashamed that she
should be tempted to yield to her desire for
reading, instead of ministering to the happiness
of her afflicted **friend.**

On her way to Mr. Ashton's, she met Janette
Gale, who ran **to** meet her, saying, "I am so
glad to meet you, I was going to your house
after you. Father and mother have gone
away, and they said I might have company
this afternoon. So I sent for Alice and Jane,
and they are coming, and I was going myself for you to make sure of you;—I am so
glad **I've met** you!—you were going to our
house was n't you?—come, I'll go right back,
and Alice and Jane are coming, and we shall
have a charming time."

Janette then stopped because she was out of
breath, and thus gave Charlotte **a** chance **to**
speak. It **was** Janette's custom to talk herself
out of breath before she made a pause, when
anything interested her strongly.

"I am much obliged to you," said Charlotte,
as soon as she obtained leave to speak; "but
I was on my way to see Susan Ashton."

"Well, no matter, you can stop and see me

4*

to-day, and go and see her some other time,"
said Janette.

"I must go and see her to-day and come
and see you some other time," said Charlotte,
smiling very sweetly.

"Our folks are not away from home every
day, and I want you to-day a great deal more
than I shall want you any other time; and Susan ·
— it wont make any difference with her."

"You forget that she has just lost her
brother, and must be very lonely. I should
like to stay with you very much, but I think I
ought to go and see poor Susan."

"You can go there to-morrow."

By this time the girls were in front of Mr.
Gale's house, and Janette took hold of Charlotte to make her come in. "Come," said
she, "you must and shall stop."

"I think I must go and see Susan; only
think how lonesome she must be."

"She is not more lonesome than I am," said
Janette, becoming vexed, and saying, as persons often do when they are vexed, what they
know is not true.

At this moment Alice and Jane were seen
coming across the fields.

"There are Alice and Jane coming, so you will not be lonely," said Charlotte.

"I don't want them," replied Janette angrily; "I want you. You are going to see Susan, because you like her better than you do me." So saying she turned and went into the house with a very red face, and a very ungraceful step.

Now it was not true that Charlotte loved Susan better than she did Janette; but Janette was certainly pursuing a course to make it true.

Charlotte was not very intimate with Susan. She did not go there very often, because there was a want of cordiality between their parents, or to speak more accurately, because Mr. Ashton did not like Mr. Gordon. The only fault he could find with him was, that he was a very zealous, godly man.

Charlotte went often to Mr. Gale's, for they were very kind and pious people, and she liked Janette because she was so ardent in whatever she undertook, as the reader will infer from what he has seen of her above. Charlotte saw that Janette had faults, but then we are very indulgent to the faults of those we love

— indeed, we are hardly willing to own that they are faults.

Charlotte was obliged to confess to herself, as she went on her way towards Mr. Ashton's, that it looked like selfishness in Janette, to desire to have her stay with her, instead of going to comfort Susan. And then what reason had she to be angry? But she soon excused it all by saying, "she wanted to see me so much that she could n't think of anything else. If she had only thought, she would not have been so selfish and hasty." This was true, but then, if she had not been selfish, her own wishes would not have so occupied her attention as to prevent her from thinking of anything else.

Charlotte found Susan very lonesome, as she had expected. She seemed very glad to see Charlotte, and so did Mrs. Ashton. Charlette did not see Mr. Ashton but once. He passed through the room on his way to his chamber, but did not seem to notice any one in the room. "Papa feels very bad," said Susan. Charlotte thought he looked as if he did.

"Did your papa and mamma ever lose a child?" said Susan.

"My little brother John died when I was very small," said Charlotte.

"What did they do?"

"I can but just remember it. They cried some, and prayed a great deal; that is the most I can remember about it."

"My papa and mamma don't pray. I don't know why. I wish they would. I guess papa is thinking about it."

This remark of Susan was overheard by Mrs. Ashton, and in connection with other thoughts which had occupied her mind, led her to resolve that it should no longer be said of her, "she does not pray."

"Susan was not much disposed to play, and it was rather hard work for Charlotte to amuse her, but she did succeed in doing so. She would now and then think of the girls who were at Mr. Gale's, and wish herself there,— but then she would check herself, and content herself with making Susan happy. Thus occupied, it was late before she started to go home.

As she passed Mr. Gale's she was in hopes of seeing Janette, and of finding her better natured, but she did not see her. Janette had finished her chapter of quarrels, by quarrelling with Alice and Jane before the afternoon was gone, thus causing them to go home. She saw Charlotte as she passed along homeward, and knew from her manner that she wished to see her, but she was not in a humor to make her appearance.

She began the afternoon in selfishness, and ended it in sorrow.

CHAPTER VIII.

THE FIRST FAMILY PRAYER.

THE next day after Charlotte's visit to Susan, an event occurred at Mr. Ashton's, which showed the correctness of Susan's surmise that her father thought of praying. Just before breakfast was ready, Mr. Ashton requested that operations might be stayed for a little while, and all his workmen called in. They came in and seated themselves with perplexed looks, which gave way to those of astonishment when Mr. Ashton came from his room with a Bible. He sat down and read with a trembling voice the third chapter of John. He then said, "let us pray." He kneeled down, and his example was followed by all his men, though he was noted for employing what was called "a hard set." The prayer offered was not after any written pattern. The forms of expression were not those commonly heard in prayer, but they were such as would leave little room to doubt that he had experienced the

change so earnestly insisted on in the chapter
named above, and one of his hearers remark-
ed, "he prayed like one that was n't used to
praying, but who **had taken** it up with all **his**
might."

"Mother," whispered Susan, after breakfast, "it seems more as it used to than it has
any time since Henry died."

Shall we follow the workmen into the field
and hear what they have to say **about the**
strange turn events have taken?

"Well," said Josiah Johns, (he **was** commonly called Siah,) when they had got a little
way from the house, on their way to the field,
and he had looked round to see that he was
not likely to be overheard, "if Ashton turns
Christian some of us had better look out."

"Why so?" said Robbins, a veteran of the
bar; "think he 'll cut us adrift?"

"I can't say how that will be, for I have n't
thought about it; but, if *he* finds it necessary
to tack about, it 's most likely it would be best
for some of us to do so. If he found he was
going the wrong way, it 's pretty clear we are
cutting it a good deal faster than he was."

"Let us see how he holds out," said Robbins;

" there are a good many who bring up for a time, and have a crying spell, and a praying spell, and then push on in their old **ways** again."

" I do n't believe," said Siah, " that it will be so with Ashton. **He** has n't gone into Christianity without considering it well, and **he** will hold on. I should like to see him give up anything he takes hold of."

" Well, we 'll see. I can't say I altogether like this leading us on, and then whipping over suddenly to the other side. I relied a good deal upon his knowledge and reasoning. I said to myself, that can't be so very necessary that squire Ashton do n't believe in at all. So I 've let the matter run along, thinking I could, **at** almost any time, bring up where he was. I do n't think I can make up my mind to go where he seems to be going now."

Robbins had no difficulty in making up his mind to follow Squire Ashton when he led him away from God and duty; why so difficult to follow **him** when he would lead him to the Lamb of God?

The reader will see from the above, what the influence of Ashton had been over those

with whom he transacted business. He had encouraged them by his example to neglect and cast off the restraints of religion. Then they often went further, and fell into vices from which he kept himself free. But for all this he was responsible, and the number who had been thus led onward towards ruin by his means, furnished a fearful comment on that passage of the Bible, " one sinner destroyeth much good."

Every one who fails to become a Christian till late in life, has a vast amount of evil to mourn over — evil which he cannot undo, and which may have already resulted in the everlasting ruin of immortal souls. Remember thy Creator in the days of thy youth. Years of danger and sorrow will thereby be escaped. Evil that can never be repaired will be avoided. A whole life spent in the service of God — in doing good — how beautiful in prospect! how delightful in reality!

CHAPTER IX.

SPIRITS WANTING IN THE HAY FIELD.

THE workmen named in the last chapter, and their companions who took no part in the conversation recorded, then proceeded to the meadow and began to lay low its glories. They worked for a long time in silence. Siah commonly led the way in talking, but he was now not disposed to talk. In most companies when the chief speaker is silent the rest follow his example. Siah was silent, because he was thoughtful, and he was thoughtful in consequence of the morning prayer.

He had been blest with a pious mother, though she was laid in her grave when he was very young. He had grown up without much religious instruction. He had become profane, a Sabbath breaker, and somewhat intemperate. Still in his heart he could never despise that religion which he was told had been the comfort of his mother during long years of poverty and desertion, and her support in death. The kind notices which he had occasionally received from Christians, for his mother's sake, had made some impression on him. Though he sat with the sinner, yet reverence for religion was sometimes felt in his heart.

The voice of prayer, from the lips of one who had encouraged him in his neglect of God, had made a deep impression on his heart. It led him to the exercise of serious and solemn thought. This, as we have said, made him silent. His companions waited in vain for the quaint and witty remark and the smart repartee that so often beguiled their labors.

"What makes you look so sober?" said one who was himself a still man, and who, like most who say but a few, observed a great many things.

"Well," said Siah, stopping and setting up his sythe for the purpose of whetting it, and as he was in front, causing all the rest to follow his example; "well," repeated he, taking off his hat, which was rather a difficult operation as it fitted his head closely and had no brim on it, and wiping his head with a sort of shred, or string, which he called a *handkercher*, "I begin to think it is a'most time to be sober."

" I guess," said Robbins, " we shall all stand a pretty good chance to be sober to-day, for I'm thinking Boss means to make praying do instead of grog. I do n't see nothing of him," looking as he had often done before for the last half hour in the direction from which Mr. Ashton was accustomed to come with a jug of spirits, for the use of his men.

The serious tone in which Siah had said " it is most time to be sober," had made such an impression, that the remark of Robbins was not followed by the expected laugh.

Before they were ready to put in their sythes again, Mr. Ashton was seen coming.

" There, it is coming," said one.

" Has he got the jug ?" said Robbins, whose sight was not as good as it would have been but for the inflammation of his eyes.

" He has got something in his hand ; I can't see just what it is."

" It is a chance," said Robbins, " if it is anything but cold water. Now days, when a man turns Christian, it is all cold water with him. It was n't so always."

" More 's the pity," said Johns.

" You think of turning cold water man ?"

" Yes."

" You don't mean to begin just yet ?" said Robbins with a sly wink to his neighbor.

" To-day."

" Not till afternoon ?"

" This forenoon."

" That's fetching it into close quarters, any how," said Robbins blowing the quid of tobacco out of his mouth that he might be ready when the jug was at hand.

He was destined to a severe disappointment. Mr. Ashton came, but instead of the jug, he brought a basket of fine bread and butter, a nice pie and several bottles of rich milk. The men seated themselves under a shady tree, and Mr. Ashton said, " My men, I can't furnish you with any more spirit ; it is not right to do so. What it has cost me shall be added to your wages in time to come ; and, if any of you have been led to neglect religion through my means, I beg that it may be so no longer. I ——" but he could say no more for weeping, and he went away, not, however, till he had noticed the tear that had started in the eye of Johns.

There was silence for some time after his departure. At last Robbins said — "You must have fixed it with Boss over night."

"No such thing," said Johns. His word was never doubted. Is that true of the reader's?

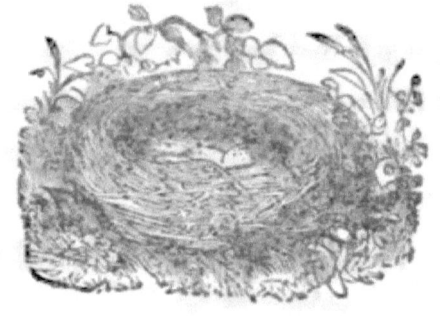

CHAPTER X.

MR. ASHTON'S VISIT TO MR. GORDON.

ONE beautiful morning Charlotte saw Mr. Ashton coming up the lane which led to her father's house. She ran to her mother and said, "Mother, Mr. Ashton is coming; what in the world do you suppose he is coming here for?"

"I do not know, but probably he wishes to see your father."

"What can he want to see him for? He do n't like father very well, you know."

By this time Mr. Ashton had reached the door.

"Is Mr. Gordon at home?" said he.

"Yes, sir," said Charlotte; "he is in the garden. Walk in, sir, and I will go and call him."

"I will go and see him in the garden," said Mr. Ashton.

He found Mr. Gordon at the farther end of the garden, leaning over the wall, with his arms resting on the top of it, looking in a direction opposite to that in which Mr. Ashton was coming. He was looking upon the landscape which lay spread out before him in great beauty, and he was thinking of the hand that had spread out that carpet of green, and painted the daisies and lilies that adorned it, and clothed the hill side with the rustling corn-hills, and the distant mountain with its firs and maples. Not knowing that any one was near him he gave utterance to his thoughts: "Wonderful! wonderful!" said the old man; "while I live I will praise the Lord."

"Amen," said a deep voice behind him. He turned quickly and saw Mr. Ashton standing near him with his outstretched hand. He took it, and a warm pressure was exchanged while Mr. Gordon scanned the countenance of his unexpected visitor. But for the tone in which the amen was uttered, he would have thought that the emotion visible in Mr. Ashton's countenance was owing to his recent bereavement, but the tone led him to suspect and hope that there was another cause.

"Come into the house," said he.

"It is pleasant here, and we are retired and alone. Let us sit down," said Mr. Ashton.

" Have you any news to tell me ?" said Mr. Gordon.

Mr. Ashton hesitated —— " Yes, I have come to tell you that I am —— " again he hesitated, and the tears came into his eyes.

" A sinner," said Mr. Gordon, supposing that was what he intended to say.

" Yes, a sinner, but I hope a converted sinner."

" You do n't say so !" said Mr. Gordon, unconsciously rising from his seat ; " is it possible ?"

He then sat down and leaned his forehead on his staff, which he held upright between his knees, and kept silence for about a minute. He was either thinking profoundly, or was engaged in prayer.

He then raised his head and began a series of questions for the purpose of obtaining a knowledge of the true state of Mr. Ashton's mind.

The late proud man patiently and cheerfully submitted to this, and made such replies as gave great joy to Mr. Gordon's heart. After a long examination he said, " I have never, in my whole life, told a person, after hearing

his experience, that I thought he was converted. I want to see how he acts as well as
how he talks. If a man is really converted
his works will show it. But now I must say,
I can't help giving you the right hand of
fellowship as a Christian brother. I can't help
thinking the Lord has wrought a work in your
soul."

Again there was a warm pressure of each
other's hands.

"You know," said Mr. Ashton, "how I
have felt towards you, and how I have treated
you."

"Why, yes, I knew you did not love me
very well, but I never had any hard thoughts
of you. It won't do for one who has to ask
forgiveness of God for as many things as I
have to, to harbor any ill will towards a fellow
being, let him do what he will. I have nothing to forgive; I hadn't before you came. I
have to forgive everybody before I go to
sleep — I couldn't go to sleep without it."

"I can readily believe you now though I
could not a few days ago."

"Now," said Mr. Gordon, "I shall believe
that the Lord can convert anybody; I am

afraid I did n't formerly think he could. Now I believe he can convert anybody, and shall take encouragement to **pray** accordingly. But how did it come to pass? I always want to hear what the Lord does, and what are the instruments he uses. I get tired of hearing of **the** great things which men do in these times, **but I never** get **tired of** hearing **what** the Lord does."

Mr. Ashton **gave him an** account of his mental history from the time of his son's death; with the outlines of this, the reader **is acquainted.**

"Life from death!" said Mr. Gordon. "God took the son to save the father." Rightfully guessing what thoughts were passing in Mr. Ashton's mind, **as** an expression of agony clouded his brow, he said, "I have been talking with James Wilson, to-day, about Henry, and I find there is very comfortable evidence to believe that the boy is with **his** Saviour."

Mr. Ashton's **look** begged for an explanation; he could not speak. Mr. Gordon then gave him an account of the facts he had learned from James in regard to Henry. Ashton was so overcome that he threw himself on his knees beside the bench on which they were sitting, and relieved his pressed heart by a whispered prayer.

When he rose from his knees and composed his countenance, Mr. Gordon said, " when I was leaning on the wall as you came, I was thinking of the wonderful power of God in creation; but that is not half as wonderful as his power and mercy in the new creation of a soul."

CHAPTER XI.

MR. ASHTON AND MR. JOHNS AT DEACON AMES' PRAYER MEETING.

THE third day after the supply of rum was stopped by Mr. Ashton, Robbins collected his tools at night, and received his pay.

"What are you going to do, Robbins?" said one of the men, seeing him shouldering his sythe, instead of hanging it for the night on the cherry tree as they were wont to do.

"I'm going to take up my line of march; I can't live on cold water. I'm not a fish."

"You get more in the increase of your wages than the liquor came to."

"I can't help that; I'm agin the principle. It is n't according to liberty. It runs right contrary to the principles of republican government. This is a free country, I reckon."

Robbins went and hired himself to a man who gave high wages, (he seldom paid them,) and very poor table fare, but as much whiskey as each one could drink. This was according to Robbins' notions of liberty. The second day he worked there, he took the liberty, when very drunk, of mowing one of his employer's legs half off, thus laming him for life.

The same evening in which Robbins took up his line of march from Mr. Ashton's, Johns lingered till after the workmen had gone to their homes. Mr. Ashton, supposing he had something he wished to say to him, went to the door. He thought it likely that Johns might be about to leave him as Robbins had done. He did not know that he had renounced rum forever.

"Well, Johns," said he, "do you think of leaving me too?"

"I wasn't thinking of any such thing. I was thinking of asking you, whether it would do to go to meeting to-night with these clothes on," looking at his coat, which had as many colors and more pieces than Joseph's of old. The meeting alluded to, was the prayer meeting which was held by deacon Ames at his house every Thursday evening, unless the pastor had a meeting on that evening.

In reply to Johns' question whether it would do to go to meeting, with the clothes he had on, Mr. Ashton said, " There will be no persons there except those whom you meet with every day, and who will be glad to see you there in any clothes."

" I should like to go," said Johns.

" I am going myself and we will go together."

Just as Mr. Ashton was ready, Mr. Gordon called. He was on his way to the meeting.

" I've stopped for you," said he to Mr. Ashton, " to go to the prayer meeting. You are going, I suppose ?"

" Yes, I was just about to set out," said Mr. Ashton.

" Here is Mr. Johns," said Mr. Gordon. He always said *Mr.* to the poor man, as well as to the rich ; " wont he go too ?"

" He was talking about going; he was rather afraid his coat would not do, but—"

" Oh, never mind that," said Gordon, interrupting Mr. Ashton ; " the Lord don't care what sort of a coat a man has, but what sort of a heart he has."

" That is the worst of it," said Johns to himself. He began to perceive the plague of his own heart.

The three went to the meeting. Those who were accustomed to meet there were mostly assembled. Several heads were dropped, as Mr. Ashton came in and took his seat beside his hired man. In course of the meeting Mr. Ashton offered a prayer, and Johns' wept very much after the fashion of a child.

At the close of the meeting, deacon Ames spoke kindly to Johns, and asked him to stop after the rest had gone.

"Your mother, Johns, used always to be at this meeting; she used to bring you in her arms."

Johns heaved a deep sigh, but made no remark.

"I had expected to see you here before this time," added the deacon.

"I do n't know what reason you had to, considering the way I've lived," said Johns.

"The reason was, I knew you had a praying mother; there is nothing equal to that in this world, you may depend upon it."

Johns heaved another and more painful sigh. He had often abused his mother's memory, because she did not marry a rich man as she once had an opportunity of doing, during her widowhood. She declined because he was an ungodly man. Johns thought if she had married she would not have left him in poverty. He now began to feel that perhaps her prayers would prove a richer legacy than all the wealth she had rejected. The remembrance of his abuse added to the burden that was weighing down his heart.

"Do n't you think," said the deacon, "that it is about time to turn about and follow your mother's footsteps?"

"I do."

"I 'm glad to hear it. The first thing you have to do is—" he hesitated.

"Leave off drinking," said Johns.

"Yes."

"I 've done that."

"That is good so far, but that is not religion."

"I know that."

"You must repent, and break off from all your sins."

"That is not so easily done. I know it ought to be done, but I do n't think I can do it."

"Why not?"

"Well, you see my mind has run in one way so long that I can't get it to run in any other.

I try to think of good things, but my mind is off in a minute to something else. I can't pray; I can't fix my mind on anything. I can't feel as I know I ought to feel."

"How came your mind to get into such a state that it wont run on anything good?"

"Because I let it run on sin for so many years."

"It is the consequence of years of wilful disobedience of God's law."

"That it is."

"Anybody to blame for that but yourself?"

"Nobody."

"When you say that you can't repent, it amounts to this then, that you are so wicked, that you can't repent."

"Yes," very despondingly.

"I do n't see as I can help you any. You must repent and believe on the Lord Jesus Christ, or you can't be saved."

"I can't repent," said Johns, shaking his head gloomily.

"Well, then, there is no hope for you, so far as I can see."

The deacon said no more to him, and he

went home with a heavier heart than he came
with.

Let the reader remember that by every
sinful act he performs, he is giving a direction
to his thoughts, which will render it more and
more difficult for him to attend to the things
which belong to his peace.

CHAPTER XII.

JAMES WILSON'S INTERVIEW WITH MR. ASHTON.

ONE day Mr. Ashton met James Wilson on his way to school. He had not spoken with him since he came to ask permission to have religious services at the funeral of Henry. Mr. Ashton's feelings were now, as you may well suppose, very warm towards James. He stopped him in the street and shook hands with him with the cordiality of an old friend.

"James," said he, "do you hold any more prayer meetings under the old oak tree?"

"No, sir, we have not lately."

"Why not?"

"Some of the boys talked so much about it and ridiculed it."

"You are too much of a man to care for that."

"I do n't care for it very much myself, but some of the rest do, and I thought it might be better not to have the meeting, than to have religion ridiculed on account of it."

" Perhaps you are right, but I doubt it. If you give no real occasion for ridicule, I would not stop for it. The very fellows that are guilty of it, are often troubled in their consciences by your persevering in what they attempt to put an end to."

James was very much pleased to talk with Mr. Ashton, or rather, to have Mr. Ashton talk to him ; but he showed signs of uneasiness at being detained, which did not escape the notice of Mr. Ashton.

" Are you in a great hurry ?" said he. " I wanted to speak with you on another subject."

" I should be very glad to talk with you, sir, but I am afraid I shall be late at school ; and though I know the teacher would excuse me, if I were to tell him you wished to see me, yet the example of being late would not be good. Our teacher says we must be careful to have our example good as well as our intentions."

" I am very glad you have so wise a teacher," said Mr. Ashton, " and I hope all his pupils will attend to his instructions as well as you do. Come and see me after school."

" I will, sir," said James. " I shall be very

happy to," and he hastened on his way, and was just in time, and not a second to spare.

There are two things noticed above, to which I wish to call the attention of the **reader.** James said he did not care *very* much for **ridicule.** He **did not deny that he did** care somewhat for it. **Most** young persons can resist **almost** any thing better than they can resist ridicule. Many have lost their souls forever, rather than endure the shafts of ridicule. But what folly, — to fear the laugh of a poor guilty sinner, more than the displeasure of a Holy God! Never suffer yourself to **be** deterred from doing what is right, through fear of being ridiculed. **Set** a double guard on this point, for it is one **of** which Satan **often** takes advantage to the ruin of the soul.

The other point **is** the regard that is to be had to our example. We may mean well, and may not do what is in itself wrong, and yet our example may be such as shall do a great deal of harm. We must take heed to our ways that we be not the occasion of leading others to do evil.

After school, James went home with little Susan. On his **way** he found, by talking with

her, that the impression made upon her mind
by Henry's death, and the events that followed
it, had almost, if not quite, passed away. This
grieved him a good deal, and made him despair
of doing her any good. When he grew older
he did not despair of doing good so readily,
but persevered in his efforts. He learned to
act in accordance with the precept, " in the
morning sow thy seed, and in the evening
withhold not thy hand : for thou knowest not
whether shall prosper either this or that, or
whether they both shall be alike good."

Mr. Ashton welcomed James very cordially,
and conversed with him for a little time in
company with Mrs. Ashton and Susan, and
then took him to his private room. He wished
to have him tell him all that had passed
between him and Henry, on the subject of
religion, and all that he knew of Henry's religious views and feelings previous to his death.
He had heard most of what James had to say,
from Mr. Gordon, but it gave him a melan-
choly pleasure to hear it again.

When James had told him all that he knew
on the subject, after a short season spent in
prayer, he went home.

Mr. Ashton, in view of what he had heard from James, respecting Henry, could not but hope that he was in heaven. Still the remembrance of that last request, " do pray for me," was like a dagger to his heart.

CHAPTER XIII.

SOME ERRONEOUS NOTIONS CORRECTED.

A GROUP of little girls, who were at Mrs. Gordon's on Saturday afternoon, were speaking of little Henry's amiable qualities, and of the hopes which were entertained, that he was now at rest.

"I do n't wish to be very good," said Eliza Green, one of the group.

"Why, Eliza! what a speech!" said Mary Ames.

"I want to be good," said Eliza, — "good enough to go to heaven if I should die; but I do n't want to be very good while I am young."

"There is nobody good enough to go to heaven," said Charlotte Gordon. "If it were not for Christ's sake, the best would not go to heaven. But I do n't see why Eliza do n't wish to be very good."

"Because," said Eliza, "very good children always die: when I read about a very good child, I always expect to come to his death."

Mrs. Gordon happening to come to the door, near which the girls were seated on the grass, overheard the last remark. She thought the mistake under which Eliza labored should be corrected. So she sat down on the door-stone, and joined in the conversation of the girls. " I think you are mistaken, Eliza, in your opinion that all very good children die young. You have not read the history of all the very good children."

" I know that, ma'am, but I have read about a great many — and they all died."

" You forget, my dear, that the history of only such as die is written. Those who are very good in childhood, and grow up to be men and women, very seldom have their lives written, or not till after they have died at the end of a long life ; and then as the events of their childhood have been in a measure forgotten, a very little space is given to them in the history."

Eliza saw that she had formed an opinion on too narrow a basis of facts. Still like older persons she was not disposed to give up her opinion without saying all she could in favor of it.

" Do n't you think," said she to Mrs. Gordon, " that very good children are more apt to
die than others ?"

" By no means.   On the contrary, I think
they are more likely to live long on the earth.
The Bible does not say that every good child
shall enjoy a long life, but it teaches that goodness has a tendency to cause length of days.
In the Psalms it is said, ' He that will love life
and see good days, let him refrain his tongue
from evil, and his lips that they speak no guile.'
Again : ' Honor thy father and thy mother,
that thy days may be long upon the land
which the Lord thy God giveth thee.'   And
again : speaking of wisdom, by which is meant
true religion, ' Length of days is in her right
hand.'   These passages and others of similar
import show that good children are more apt
to live than others."

" Are not very bright children apt to
die ?" said one of the girls.

" You do not use the word bright in its true
sense.   *Precocious* is the word that expresses
your meaning.   Such children are very apt to
die.   The activity of their minds is owing to
a diseased state of the brain, or rather, in such

cases, the brain grows more rapidly than the rest of the body, and thereby becomes diseased, and persons seldom recover from diseases of the brain. A precocious child, one whose mind opens too fast, one whose mind ripens too soon, is very different from a good child. There is nothing in goodness which tends to shorten life, but on the contrary, goodness, as we have seen, tends to lengthen life."

"There is no reason then, Eliza," said one, " why you should not wish to be *very* good."

" When you say," said Mrs. Gordon, " that you do n't wish to be very good, it is the same as saying you do n't wish to be very happy. Is it true that you do n't wish to be happy ?"

" No, ma'am," said Eliza, in some surprise at Mrs. Gordon's remark. " I know we must be good in order to be happy, but — I did n't think we must be very good. I thought, —" and she hesitated to express her opinion for some reason.

" What did you think ?" said Mrs. Gordon with an encouraging smile.

" I thought that *very* good people were not so happy as —"

" As those who are only pretty good."

" Yes, ma'am."

Strange as it may seem, Mrs. Gordon saw by the looks of the girls that there were several, at least, who agreed in opinion with Eliza.

" What reasons have you for such an opinion ?" said Mrs. Gordon.

" When persons are very good they have to give up a great many things which are pleasant, and to do a great many things that are not pleasant. So they can't be so happy as those who do n't have to do so."

" Give me an example of what you mean by saying a very good person must give up many pleasant things."

" Why, if a person is very pious he must deny himself and take up his cross, and must never do anything for pleasure."

" Be a little more particular; name some pleasant thing, something that contributes to real happiness, that a very pious person must give up."

" Well, he must not go on pleasure excursion — must not go a sailing on the lake. Last week, when we went from Mr. James' and sailed up and down for pleasure, I am sure we were all very happy. Well, Mr. Stokes, at the prayer meeting, said that Christians must deny themselves — that they must not go sailing for pleasure, but must take up their cross. He meant to reprove Mr. and Mrs. James, I suppose, as they were the only professors of religion in the boat."

" Was the sailing excursion you speak of on the Sabbath ?"

" Oh, no, indeed! it was on Saturday afternoon, when Mr. and Mrs. James said they had got their work ' done up, ready for the Sabbath.' "

" Was there anything wrong then in the excursion or in anything about it."

" No, ma'am, if there had been, I do n't think Mr. James would have gone."

" Why then must a very pious person avoid sailing for pleasure ? According to your view, it would seem that to be pious at all, it is necessary to avoid every thing that is wrong; but to be very pious, it is necessary to avoid some things that are not wrong. To be pious is to do right ; to be very pious is to do more than right! Do you find the Bible teaching any such doctrine ?"

"The Bible says we must deny ourselves and take up our cross."

"True it does, and this command rests on all Christians, the pious as well as the very pious. It commands us to deny ourselves every thing that is wrong, and to do every thing which is right, however crossing to our sinful inclinations it may be. That is what is meant by denying ourselves and taking up our cross. The more pious any one is, the more like God he is, and the more happy he is. Thus to be very good is to be very happy."

"I suppose it must be so, but I always thought that it was otherwise."

"Mrs. Gordon," said one of the little girls who was much more interested in the former part of the conversation, "why do so many children die?"

"I cannot tell," said Mrs. Gordon, "what are the reasons of God's dealings, when he does not reveal them. Death has passed upon all men for all have sinned. If children were not sinners they would not die. Perhaps one reason why death takes the young as well as the old is that all may feel their danger, and refrain from sin, and prepare for death."

"Why did the Lord make Henry Ashton die?" said another little girl.

"I have said, my dear, that I cannot tell the reasons of God's doings, when he does not reveal them. We ought to be very careful about assigning reasons for the Divine conduct when He does not assign them. But we. can see the effects that have followed an act, and may say, probably the accomplishment of these effects, was one of the purposes of God in doing the act. Now in regard to our dear little Henry's death, we can see what effects have followed. There is the hopeful conversion of his father and mother, and Mr. Johns, all of whom you know intend soon to make a profession of religion. Probably one part of God's design in taking Henry away was to produce these effects. Another object God may have had in view was to warn his young companions, and to cause them to prepare for eternity." She dwelt on this thought solemnly and tenderly for a little space, till many of her auditors were in tears.

CHAPTER XIV.

THE CHURCH MEETING.

AT a meeting of the church called for the purpose of examining candidates for admission, Mr. Ashton related his experience. It was known that he intended to do so, and the meeting was in consequence fully attended. He gave some account of his childhood, which was not blessed by a pious mother's care. He gave some account of the causes that led him into infidelity, and of his hours of anguish while in that dreadful state. He described the feelings he had entertained towards zealous Christians, and his efforts to baffle all their attempts to do him good. He told of the dying words of his first born; of the cold, stern agony that took up its abode in his unrelenting heart; of the fruitless visit of deacon Ames; of the successful one of James and George. He described the impression of the pastor's address, and prayer, the more powerful, because not directly addressed to his conscience; his impulse to see the prayer meeting, his unobserved attendance and its effects; the struggles of his soul, till he was enabled to commit his all into the hands of the Saviour, through whose merits he professed to indulge a humble hope, and whose name he now wished to profess before men.

During his remarks there was death-like silence in the crowded room, and tears ran silently down many a cheek, but when he closed by the simple expression of his faith, and his desire to cast in his name with those who look for salvation to Christ's blood alone, there was audible sobbing in every part of the room.

Mr. Johns then related his experience. He made his appearance in clean and neatly-patched clothes, for since his reformation the affection of his wife had revived, and his home was neat and comfortable as of old. He gave his history at greater length than Mr. Ashton had done, with more repetition, and less accuracy of expression, yet it was scarcely less interesting. Soul-history, as deacon Ames was wont to say, is the most interesting of all history. Those who were present at that meeting did not differ from him in opinion.

Johns ascribed the seriousness that led to his conversion to the first family prayer of Mr. Ashton, and to his subsequent conduct. A very few questions were asked him, and he with Mr. and Mrs. Ashton, who had previously been examined by a committee of the Church, were received as candidates for admission to the Church, after the usual period had intervened.

Mr. Rockwell was at the meeting and was deeply affected among the rest. It will be recollected that Mr. Rockwell was a good deal concerned about the prayer meeting under the old oak tree. After meeting, deacon Ames happened to be walking by the side of Mr. Rockwell. The deacon had seen the feeling manifested by him during the meeting, and hence thought he would make a remark which might be profitable.

" Well," said he kindly, " the boys' prayer meeting in the wood turned out better than we expected."

" It turned out better than I expected. I wish there was one there to-night, for me to go to. I am afraid there is something in religion, that I do n't know anything about."

"It is a great matter to build on the true foundation. We can never see to it too carefully that we have the right spirit, — that we are resting on Christ's merits, and are doing his will."

8

CHAPTER XV.

JAMES WILSON IN GREAT PERIL.

THE connexion which James and George had with Mr. Ashton's change of views and feeling, of the subject of religion, was the subject on much conversation, after what had occurred at the church meeting, described in the last chapter. A good deal was said to the boys about it, in the way of praise, especially to James, who seemed to have had more influence with Mr. Ashton than George had, or at least was mentioned by him more frequently.

The watchful pastor foresaw the bad effects which this injudicious praise might have on his beloved boys, and did what he could to prevent it by seeing them, and trying to put them on their guard against pride, especially in that worst of its forms, spiritual pride. He reminded them that they were only instruments in the Divine hand; that they ought to be very thankful for being made instruments of good, instead of displeasing God by claiming the honor due to him alone. George listened to his remarks with earnest, and James with respectful attention.

The truth was that James was a little lifted up by the results connected with his efforts, and thought that the good pastor, in talking to him as he did, regarded him too much as a little child. He thought that he was not in as much danger as Mr. Jones seemed to think he was.

In a day or two after this interview, he resolved to go and see Susan, and do what he could for her. In his secret heart, he felt as though he could do a little more towards making her religious than anybody else could.

He found her quite indifferent to the subject of religion. She also showed but little feeling when mention was made of Henry's death. James became vexed that she should pay so little attention to what he said, and evince so little feeling. He made some rather severe remarks, which made her angry, and provoked her to say, " My father do n't get angry since he has become a Christian." This was regarded by James as an implied assertion that he was not a Christian, and it did not add to his meekness.

When he left her, he was in a very differ‑
ent mood from that in which he left the old
oak **tree,** after the prayer meeting; and the
school-house, when a railing accusation was
brought against him — times which the reader
will well recollect. If any one had told him
then, that he would ever feel as he did, when
he turned away from Susan, would he have
believed it? No. This passage in his history
was another illustration **of** the truth **that** "**the**
heart is deceitful above all things," and another
admonition to give heed **to** the precept, "let
him that thinketh he standeth, take heed lest
he fall."

"I will never try to do her any good again,"
said James to himself on his way home. "It
is of no use, she is so hard hearted."

Before he got home he fell in with George.

"Where have you been?" said George.

"I have been to see Susan Ashton, and I
shall not go again."

"I would n't say so," said George, soothing‑
ly, for he saw that he was disturbed in spirit.

"I am tired trying to do her any good, she
has so little feeling."

"She has n't a great deal, but you must

remember that she has not had very good instruction."

" Her father is pious now."

" I trust he is, but I heard him say it was awkward for him to teach others, especially his own child, the things he had so long despised."

George saw that his friend was in a very unhappy state of mind, and brought the conversation to a close as soon as he could. He thought that time and reflection would be more likely to bring James right than anything he could say.

The result showed the wisdom of George's course. It is seldom wise to reprove a friend when his mind is disturbed by passion. It is generally best to wait till he has become perfectly cool.

At night when James came to review the events of the day, he found that his visit to Susan formed by no means a pleasant picture in his memory. The expression made to himself and repeated in substance to George, — " I will never try to do her any good again," — was distinctly remembered. It seemed to stay before his mind for the purpose of inviting reflection. Reflections such as these came to

his mind.   How many years God endured my
indifference and perverseness, and never said,
" I will never try to do him any good again."
He remembered how many warnings and invita-
tions and appeals God had caused to be made
to him, and though he gave little or no heed to
them, yet the arm of mercy was outstretched
still, and the goodness of God poured around
him to lead him to repentance. He remembered that when he was brought to repentance
it was God's act, making him willing in the
day of his power. He saw that in his own
dealings with Susan he had come far short of
following God's dealings with him. He inquired why it was that he had been led to
forget himself so as to yield to such feelings,
and give utterance to such expressions. He
saw that he had been puffed up by the
praises of those who had ascribed to him so
much in the conversion of Mr. Ashton. He
saw that he had exalted himself before God,
and that it was meet that he should be humbled.
He was humbled and penitent. He wept and
prayed for forgiveness. He went and made
confession to his pastor for his inattention to his
advice. He went to George and took back

the hasty words he had spoken in his hearing. He went to Susan with a spirit of humility and tenderness which deeply touched her heart, and entirely removed the unfavorable influence his previous visit had excited.

Thus happily his early repentance prevented the great evil which would have been occasioned had his fall been known to those who watch for occasions to reproach religion.

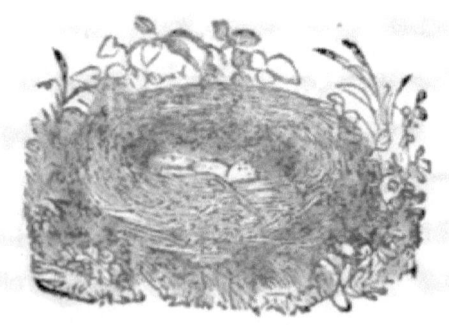

CHAPTER XVI.

THE PUBLIC PROFESSION — SCENE IN THE GRAVE-YARD.

A GREAT crowd assembled in the meeting house, when Mr. Ashton was to be admitted to the church. The late scornful sinner stood meekly in the aisle, and before men pledged himself to be a follower of that Saviour whom he had so openly despised. Beside him stood his wife and Mr. Johns. The employer and the employed were on equality before God. They felt that they were brethren in Christ.

Little Susan was in Mr. Ashton's pew alone. She could not join with her parents in consecrating herself to God ; but many a prayer was breathed for her to Him who had done so much for the family to which she belonged.

The tears that dimmed the father's eye as he stood in that aisle, were caused by the thought that his darling child was in bondage to sin, and that his former influence had perhaps riveted the chains.

When the services of the day were over, two aged women were seen lingering in a distant corner of the grave-yard which was adjacent to the church. They were widows, and they had gone thither to weep; the one, over the remains of the companion of her pilgrimage, and the other, over those of her son, who had been the stay of her old age. They were intimate friends, for they were devoted followers of the same master. As they were leaving the grave-yard, they met and stood in silence for a moment over the grave of Henry, which was near the gate.

"Well," said one, "I never expected to see this day. Little Henry I used to love, and I classed him among my hopeful ones, and when he was taken away, I thought he was taken away from the evil that was to come; but we little know what God intends to do."

"I always hoped to see Mr. Ashton brought in."

"Did you?"

"Yes. I used to know his aunt, who was a very good woman, and prayed for him a great deal; and she told me his grandmother and grandfather were among the excellent of the earth, and prayed almost without ceasing for their children; so that I can't say I never expected to see this day; but it is a wonderful mercy."

"There is poor little Susan left. I hope she will not stay away and be left behind, when her parents and brother enter through the gates into the city."

Over the grave of the first born, they breathed a prayer for the surviving child, and retired to their lonely dwellings.

TAKING HIM IN HAND.

"Isaac," said George, "why don't you take that fellow in hand; he has insulted you almost every day for a week."

"I mean to take him in hand," said Isaac.

"I would make him stop if I had to take his ears off."

"I mean to make him stop."

"Go and flog him now. I should like to see you do it. You can do it easily enough with one hand."

"I rather think I could; but I shan't try it to-day."

This conversation took place between two boys as they were on their way home from school. At this point in the conversation their roads led them in different directions.

The boy alluded to was the son of an intemperate man, who was angry with Isaac's father in consequence of some effort to prevent his obtaining rum. The drunkard's **son** took up the cause of **his** father, and called Isaac hard names every time he saw him pass, and as he did not do any thing by **way of retaliation, he** went farther and threw stones at him.

Isaac **was** at first provoked at the boy's con-duct. He thought he ought to be thankful that his father was checked in any measure in pro-curing rum, — the source of so much misery to himself **and** family. But when he thought of the way in which he had been brought up, his ignorance and wretchedness, he pitied him, and ceased to wonder or to be offended with his conduct. He resolved, indeed, to "take him in hand," and to "stop him," but not in the sense in which his school-fellow understood **those** terms.

The boy's name was James, but he was never **called** anything but Jim. Indeed, if you were to call him by his true name, **he** would think you meant somebody else.

The first opportunity Isaac had of taking him in hand was on election day. On that day as Isaac was on his way home, he saw a group of boys a little off the road, and heard some shouting and laughing. Curiosity led him to the spot. He found that the group were gathered around Jim and another boy a good deal larger than he was. This boy was making fun of Jim's clothes, which were indeed very ragged and dirty, and telling how he must act to become as distinguished a man as his father. Jim was very angry, but when he attempted to strike his persecutor, he would take hold of Jim's hands, and he was so much stronger that he could easily hold them. Jim then tried kicking, but as he was barefoot, he could not do much execution in that line; besides, while he was using one foot in this way, his tormentor would tread on the other one with his heavy boot.

When Isaac came up and saw what was going on, he remonstrated with the boys for countenancing such proceedings; and such was his influence, and the force of truth, that most of them agreed that it was " too bad ;" though he was such an " ugly dog," they said, that he was hardly worth pitying.

The principal actor, however, did not like Isaac's interference, but he soon saw that Isaac was not afraid of him, and that he was too popular with the other boys to be made the object of abuse. As he turned to go away, he said to Jim : " I 'll keep my eye upon you, and when you go home I 'll go with you. It is on my way, and I 'll keep off the crows ; they shant hurt you ; so do n't cry any more."

" Come, Jim, go home with me ; I 'm going now," said Isaac.

Jim did not look up or make any answer. He did not know what to make of Isaac's behavior towards him. It could not be because he was afraid of him and wished to gain his good will, for he was not afraid of one that was much stronger than he. He had never heard of the rule, " Love your enemies ; do good to those who hate you ;" for he had never been to Sabbath school, and could not read the Bible, for he did not know his letters.

He followed silently and sullenly, pretty near to Isaac, till he reached home, if that sacred name can with propriety be applied to the wretched abode of sin and misery.

He parted from Isaac without thanking him for his good offices in his behalf. This Isaac did not wonder at, considering the influences under which he had grown up. That he parted with him without abusing him, Isaac considered as something gained.

The next morning George and Isaac met on their way to school. As they passed the drunkard's dwelling, Jim was at the door, but he did not look up or say anything as they passed. He looked very much as though he had been whipped. George did not know what had taken place the day before. " What keeps Jim so still," said he.

" Oh ! I 've had him in hand."

" Have you ! I 'm glad of it. When was it ?"

" Yesterday."

" At election ?"

" Yes."

" Anybody see you do it ?"

" Yes ; some of the boys."

" Found it easy enough ; did n't you ? Did you give him enough to stop him ?"

" I guess so ; he is pretty still this morning you see."

Upon the strength of this conversation, George circulated a report that Isaac had flogged Jim. This created a good deal of surprise, as it was not in keeping with Isaac's character. The report at length reached the ears of the teacher. He inquired about the matter of Isaac, and laughed heartily when he learned in what manner George had been deceived, or rather had deceived himself. He warmly commended Isaac for his new mode of taking his enemies in hand, and advised him to continue to practise it.

A few days afterwards, as Isaac was on his way to school, he met Jim driving some cattle to a distant field. The cattle were very unruly, and Jim made very little headway with them. First one would run back, and then another, till he began to despair of being able to drive them to the pasture. He burst out crying, and said, "Oh dear! I can't make them go, and father will kill me if I do n't."

Isaac pitied his distress, and volunteered to assist him. It cost him a good deal of running and kept him from school nearly all the morning. When the cattle were safe in the pasture, Jim said, "I shan't stone you any more."

"I do n't think you will," said Isaac, smiling.

When he reached the school-house he showed signs of the violent exercise he had been taking. "What has Isaac been about?" was the whispered question which went round. When put to him he replied, "I have been chasing cattle to pasture." He was under stood to mean his father's cattle.

After school, he waited till all the pupils had left the school room before he went up to the teacher to give his excuse for being late at school.

" What made you so late ?" said the teacher.

" I was taking Jim in hand again, sir ;" and he gave him an account of his proceeding, adding at the close, "I thought you would excuse me, sir."

" Very well ; you are excused."

Reader! if you have enemies who annoy you, *take them in hand* in the same way that Isaac did, and you will be certain, if you persevere, to *stop them*.

CRUELTY TO

THE FATHERLESS BOY.

"Come on," said one of a group of boys, just dismissed from school; "let us bring snow from that bank and cover this steep place, and we can slide ever so far."

All assented to this proposal, but there was a difficulty in the want of tools. They loaded their sleds with snow with their hands and feet, but this was a slow operation. Charles found a thin piece of board, which he used for a shovel.

"Let me have it," said James. Charles saw no reason why he should do so, and kept on using it himself. James then threw a large handful of snow in his face, saying, "take that then."

This caused Charles to drop the board in order to wipe his face. Another boy snatched it up.

" Please give me my shovel," said Charles.

" You threw it away, and now you shall not have it."

" Take that," **said James**, hitting Charles with a snowball.

" **Give it to him**," shouted Sammy, a very small boy, following the example of James; **and** this **was** followed by **a** general attack. Charles was provoked at this unjust treatment, and was at first disposed to avenge himself; but certain thoughts came into his mind, which led him to drop the snowball **he had** formed, and walk **away towards his home.**

" He is going to tell his father," said one, in a taunting tone.

" He has n't got any father," said another, in a triumphing tone.

Charles turned towards the last speaker, with a look of sadness and sorrow, such as seldom shades the countenance **of** a boy of ten. **But** it had no effect, save on a small boy of seven years old, who had not joined in the attack. He **ran** after Charles, and as he happened to have a snowball in his hand, the boys supposed he was going to throw it at Charles.

" Give it to him, Will," said the brutal boy

(for he deserved no better name) who said "he has n't got any father." Willy's indignation was so great that he turned and threw the snowball at him; it struck him on the nose. He then ran and overtook Charles. "I 'm going home with you," said he to Charles, in a tone which showed how fully he sympathized with him. Charles took him by the hand, and they walked on in silence; when Willy, seeing that he was weeping, asked " Did they hurt you ?"

" No, I do n't care for snowballs; but I have nobody to care for me; my father is in **his** grave."

" But your uncle is good to you ?"

" Oh yes, very; but then he can't talk to children, nor feel for them. He means to be **very kind,** and **he is,** only I feel very sad when I think of father."

Charles was the only son of a very kind father, who had died about six months before the occurrence of the incident above **related.** Charles was then sent far away from his native place, to live with his uncle. His uncle and aunt pitied him, and loved him, and wished to make him happy. But they had no children of their own, and did not know how to sympathize with him. Their habits and manners were very different from those to which he had been accustomed. Everything was unlike his own home. He felt very lonely and unhappy, but tried to conceal it from his kind benefactors. He did not enjoy playing with the boys of the village much. At first they were all strangers; and they were often rude to him, though he was very careful to avoid giving any just cause of offence.

Willy spent an hour with Charles at his uncle's, and when he went home, told his mother how the boys had treated Charles.

"I am glad you acted as you did," said his mother, "except in one thing. Always take the part of the injured, my son."

"I always mean to, ma'am."

"Don't you suppose you are a great deal happier than if you had joined with the wicked boys?"

"I know I am, ma'am. But what was the one thing you meant, mother?"

"You should not have thrown the snow-ball at Thomas."

"Why, mother, he was so provoking that I could not help it. I think he deserved it."

"I know he deserved to be punished, but you were not the person to punish him. While it was proper that you should feel indignant at his unfeeling conduct, yet it should not have led you to do an angry act. 'Vengeance is mine, I will repay, saith the Lord.'"

"I know that, mother. Charles said he was tempted to flog James when he threw snow in his face; but then he remembered what his father said to him."

"What was it?"

"He said, a little while before he died, his father took him into a room alone, and told him he would n't have a father long; and told him what he wanted him to do when he was gone. He told him never to omit reading a chapter in the Bible and prayer every day, and to treat his mother kindly, and take care of her if he ever got old enough, and never to return evil for evil."

"He might have gone farther, and told him to return good for evil, after the manner of Him who said, 'Love your enemies, do good to them that hate you, and pray for them that despitefully use you and persecute you.'"

"I guess he did tell him so, mother; for

when I asked him if he ever meant to speak to Thomas again, he said he should speak to him, just as if nothing had happened, and that he should pray for him when he went to bed."

" He is a noble boy, and one that, if I were you, I should be proud to call my friend."

" I like him better than I do any of the rest of the boys. He never runs over the little boys. All the boys push little Sammy around, only Charles; and do n't you think, mother, little Sam was among the first that cried out, ' give it to him ?' "

" That was very naughty. But boys and men often act in that way."

" If I were Charles, I would not do any thing for him again."

" My dear, do n't say so ; that is not the right spirit. I have no doubt, from what I hear of Charles, that he will continue to treat Sammy well. He does not deserve it, to be sure. He should be kindly treated, because it is the command of God. What if God were to treat you, as you say you would treat Sammy, if you were Charles ? God has done a great deal for you, given you a happy home, kind friends, means of education, ten thousand blessings,— and yet you have not been thankful, you have disobeyed Him, you have treated Him far worse than Sammy has treated Charles, and yet He continues his goodness. He is kind to the unthankful. Much more should we sinners be so."

THE END.

www.ingramcontent.com/pod-product-compliance
Lightning Source LLC
Chambersburg PA
CBHW022142020726
47496CB00008B/2523